ON MY HONOR

YEARLING BOOKS are designed especially to entertain and enlighten young people. Patricia Reilly Giff, consultant to this series, received her bachelor's degree from Marymount College and a master's degree in history from St. John's University. She holds a Professional Diploma in Reading and a Doctorate of Humane Letters from Hofstra University. She was a teacher and reading consultant for many years, and is the author of numerous books for young readers.

ON MY HONOR

MARION DANE BAUER

A YEARLING BOOK

Published by
Bantam Doubleday Dell Books for Young Readers
a division of
Bantam Doubleday Dell Publishing Group, Inc.
1540 Broadway
New York, New York 10036

This book was written before bicycle safety helmets were widely worn.

ISBN: 0-440-46633-4

Reprinted by arrangement with Houghton Mifflin Company

Printed in the United States of America

October 1987

35 34 33 32 31

OPM

For the Mason family,
whose lives formed
part of the fabric of my childhood

CHAPTER ONE

"CLIMB THE STARVED ROCK BLUFFS? YOU'VE gotta be kidding!" Joel's spine tingled at the mere thought of trying to scale the sheer river bluffs in the state park. He looked Tony square in the eye. "Somebody got killed last year trying to do that! Don't you remember?"

Tony shrugged, popped a wheelie on his battered BMX, spun in place. "Nobody knows if that guy was really trying to climb the bluffs. He might have fallen off the top . . . or even jumped."

Joel bent over his Schwinn ten-speed and brushed imaginary dust off the fender. "Well, I'm not going to ride out there with you if that's what you're going to do. It's dumb." He tried to sound tough, sure of himself. Maybe, for once, he would be able to talk Tony out of one of his crazy ideas.

"You don't have to climb if you're scared, Bates," Tony said.

"Who's scared?" Joel licked his lips, which seemed to have gone dry. "I'd just rather go swimming, that's all. It's going to be a scorcher today. Or we could work on our tree house. My dad got us some more wood."

"We can do the tree house later," Tony said, "after we get back. And I don't feel like swimming."

"You never feel like swimming," Joel muttered, seeing in his mind the shining blue water of the municipal pool. The truth was, Tony rarely felt like doing anything that Joel wanted to do. Joel wondered, sometimes, why they stayed friends. There had to be something more than their having been born across the street from each other twelve years ago, their birthdays less than a week apart.

Mrs. Zabrinsky, Tony's mother, started baby-sitting Joel after his mother went back to work when he was six months old, so he and Tony had spent their baby years drooling on the same toys. Now Joel just checked in with her during the day, let her know where he was going, things like that. But he didn't know what kept him and Tony together except that, after Tony, other kids seemed boring.

"Come on, Joel," Tony said. "Ride out to the park with me today, and tomorrow I'll go swimming with you."

Joel thought of the long, curving, watery slide at the pool. He sighed. Tomorrow it would probably rain. Or Tony would have some other plan . . . as crazy as this one. He would pretend he had forgotten he promised to go to the pool. Joel resettled his lunch in the saddlebag behind his bicycle seat. It wasn't much fun to go swimming alone, but still it would be better than getting killed on the park bluffs. There were signs all over warning people to stay on the paths, and Tony wanted to climb from the river side, no less.

The front door of Joel's house opened and his father came out with Bobby, Joel's four-year-old brother. Mrs. Zabrinsky was Bobby's baby-sitter now, and their father was always the one to give Bobby his breakfast and take him to the Zabrinskys' house because their mother had to leave for work earlier than he.

Seeing his father and the firm grip he maintained on Bobby's hand gave Joel an idea. He would ask for permission to ride his bike out to Starved Rock.

He wouldn't mention about the bluffs, of course. He wouldn't have to. His father was sure to say that the ride to the park was too far, too dangerous. His dad always worried about things like that. Tony would be mad that he had asked, but they were *supposed* to ask, after all. At least Tony wouldn't be able to say that Joel had stayed home because he was chicken.

"Hi, Dad," Joel called. This was going to be easy. "Can I bike out to Starved Rock with Tony?" He turned his back slightly to Tony to avoid seeing what he knew would be a dirty look.

His father stopped and squinted against the morning sun that had just risen above the houses across the street. "All the way out to the state park?" he repeated, as though there were some other Starved Rock in Illinois.

"Yeah," Joel said. "It's not so far. Probably only ten or twelve miles."

"More like eight or nine, I think," his father said, approaching with Bobby in tow, "but it's still a long ride."

"I wanna go, too," Bobby announced. "I wanna go to the park. Can I, Daddy? Can I, Joel?" His voice reminded Joel of the hovering whine of a mosquito. Their mother said whining was a stage all four-year-olds went through. Joel thought a year was a long stage.

"It's a hot day," his father continued, ignoring Bobby's plea, "and that road is awfully narrow . . . hilly and winding, too."

"Can I, Daddy?" Bobby's voice rose in volume and pitch. "Can I go with Joel?"

"No." Their father shook his head. "I'm not even sure these two are going anywhere. Now, you run across to the Zabrinskys. But be careful, Bobby! Watch for cars!"

There were almost no cars to watch for on their quiet street, but their father always said things like that anyway. Bobby went, his lower lip sticking out like a shelf.

"We'll be careful, Dad." Joel could hear the whine in his own voice. He sounded almost as bad as Bobby. He sounded as if he really wanted to go.

"We will, Mr. Bates. Honest!" Tony pleaded. "The park's not that far . . . and there's not much traffic during the week."

Joel's father ran his fingers through his hair, leaving it standing on end. "I know the traffic is sparse, but with all those hills . . . it'll seem like a lot farther."

"If we get tired, we'll just turn back," Tony said.

Joel didn't say anything more. To win this argument would be to lose. He was sure, though, that his father wasn't going to give permission.

His father surveyed their bikes, frowning slightly. Joel wondered if he was going to ask why Tony was carrying a rope looped over his handlebars. *To tie ourselves together when we climb,* Tony had announced. But Joel's father merely said, "You have lunches packed already?"

"Sure," Tony answered, patting the lunch he had tied to his handlebars with the rope.

Joel's father turned back to him. "You know you have your paper route to do this afternoon, Joel."

Joel nodded. He knew. Maybe *that* would be an excuse.

"What if you boys get too tired to ride back? Tony's mother doesn't have a car, and I don't want anybody to have to leave work to come after you."

Tony was looking at Joel, obviously waiting for him to play out his side of the argument.

"We won't get tired," Joel said automatically.

His father's eyes seemed to know better, but he turned to Tony and asked, "Does your mother know what you're planning to do?"

"Sure," Tony answered cheerfully, and Joel knew,

without even checking Tony's face, that he was lying. He never told his mother anything if he could help it, and she was so busy with the littler kids that she didn't ask many questions.

His father merely accepted Tony's word with a nod – grown-ups could be really dense sometimes – but then he almost redeemed himself by suggesting, "How about trying the county road that goes out of town the other way? It's flat and would be easier riding."

"It doesn't go anywhere," Tony complained. "Besides, it's boring. Nothing but cornfields on every side."

No bluffs to climb, Joel added silently.

Joel's father sighed, buttoned his suit jacket, and then unbuttoned it again. The sigh gave Joel's stomach a small twist. His father wasn't actually considering giving permission, was he? Tony's father would have answered in a second. He would have said, "No!"

"What do you think, son?" his father asked. "Do you really think you can make it all the way to the park and back without any trouble?"

Joel could feel Tony watching him, waiting. "Sure," he said, though his throat seemed to tighten around the word. "It'll be a cinch."

7

Joel's father shook his head. "I doubt that, but I guess it won't hurt you boys to be good and tired tonight."

Joel's knees went watery. His father was going to say they could go!

"We'll build up the muscles in our legs," Tony announced, jubilant.

Joel's father didn't take his eyes off Joel's face. "On your honor?" he said. "You'll watch for traffic, and you won't go anywhere except the park? You'll be careful the whole way?"

"On my honor," Joel repeated, and he crossed his heart, solemnly, then raised his right hand. To himself, he added, *The only thing I'll do is get killed on the bluffs, and it'll serve you right.*

His father looked at him for a long moment; then he nodded his head. "Okay," he said. "I guess you're old enough now for a jaunt like this."

"Put her there, man," Tony exclaimed, holding a grubby palm toward Joel, and then he added, "I get dibs on the Schwinn!"

Joel gave Tony five, taking in his friend's face as he did. Tony's dark eyes were bright with laughter, with fun, and he was grinning like a circus clown. Joel shook his head. "How can you get dibs on *my* bike?" he asked, though he knew how. When you were Tony, the outrageous seemed natural.

His father was still watching him, so Joel added, automatically, "Thanks, Dad." He tried to sound as though he were really glad. He even forced a smile, though his mouth felt stiff. "Thanks a lot."

His father nodded again, his face remaining serious. "Remember, son," he said one last time, "you're on your honor."

"Sure," Joel replied. The least his father could have done was to remind them about staying off the bluffs. "I know."

CHAPTER TWO

JOEL WATCHED HIS FATHER DRIVE AWAY. HE felt betrayed, trapped. How could he explain to Tony that he had been kidding, that he had never had any intention of going with him to the park once the idea of climbing the bluffs had come up?

"Can I ride your bike, Joel?" Tony begged. "Can I, huh?"

Joel sighed. Tony was like a kid expecting Christmas, not someone about to risk his life. "Just for the ride out," he said. When they came back — *if* they came back — he knew he would be glad for the gears on the Schwinn to make the ride easier.

Tony's bike was a hand-me-down that had belonged to three older brothers before it had come to be his. There were no fenders, no handlegrips, and only a few flecks left of the original red paint. It was perfect for wheelies, though, and for going off ramps. Joel's silver ten-speed could be ridden fast or it could be ridden slowly, but it wasn't good for anything else.

Joel reached over to take hold of Tony's bike, supporting his own for Tony at the same time. "Come on," he said. "Let's go."

It took only about ten minutes to reach the edge of town. On their way past the school, Tony stuck out his tongue in the direction of the sixth grade classroom where they had spent last year. Joel, deciding he might as well get into the spirit of the day, followed suit, though he liked school well enough.

The sun sizzled in a sky so blue it could have been created out of a paint can. When they left the town behind, they rode between stands of tall, whispering grass rising on each side of the highway. Meadowlarks called from the ditch banks.

Tony's exuberance knew no bounds. He rode in figure eights or in circles that occupied both lanes of the nearly deserted highway. Once he tried a square and nearly toppled off Joel's bike.

Joel moved ahead, and when he started down the hill into the Vermillion River valley, he leaned forward and pumped, pushing Tony's old bike until it hummed. This was the first of many valleys they would encounter, and Joel knew going up the other side would be tough. Maybe, he thought, with a sudden rush of hope, Tony would get tired before they got all the way to the park.

Soon the bike was going faster than he could pump, so he had to let it coast. Still it gathered speed. He tried, once, to glance over his shoulder to see how close behind Tony was following. His front wheel wobbled dangerously when he turned his head, though, so he kept his eyes forward, concentrating on keeping the wheel still. His tires buzzed against the smooth blacktop, and the wind swept through his hair, holding it back from his face as if by strong fingers. It forced his eyelids open and made his eyes feel dry and crackly.

By the time Joel got to the bridge, the lowest point between the two hills, he would be flying. With the speed he had built up, he figured he could be halfway up the other side before he had to get off to push.

Joel reached the bottom of the hill and shot across the bridge so fast that he didn't get even a glimpse of the river below. He knew exactly how it would look, though, muddy red with lazy, oily-looking swirls. As soon as the bike's momentum slowed enough that his legs could keep pace with the spinning wheels, he started pumping, measuring his distance on the upward side, standing when the pumping began to get hard so he could force each pedal down with all his weight.

When his legs began to feel rubbery, he climbed off and started pushing. Tony would probably pass him, still riding the Schwinn.

"That was some hill, huh?" He tossed the words over his shoulder. Getting no answer, he turned around to see where Tony was.

Tony was at the bottom of the hill in the middle of the bridge, the Schwinn leaning carelessly against the fat iron railing. He was hanging a long way out over the railing, peering down at the river.

"Bummer!" Joel said and, glancing up and down the highway to check for cars — even when he was mad at his father he couldn't help doing things like that — he U-turned, climbed back on, and began coasting again. Next time he wouldn't get more than a few feet trying to start up from a dead stop at the bottom. He would have to walk the entire hill. But of course Tony didn't think of things like that. Maybe it was time they traded bikes back again.

_____

"What're you looking at?" he asked, as he popped a wheelie and spun next to Tony.

"The river," Tony replied, leaning out even farther. "I'm looking at Old Man River."

"No, you're not. Old Man River is the Mississippi. That's nothing but the Vermillion down there."

Tony didn't answer. Joel knew his correction didn't matter to Tony. If he wanted to call the Vermillion Old Man River, he would. He was that way in school, too . . . even on tests. He drove the teachers nuts.

Looking at Tony leaning over the railing like some kind of acrobat on a trapeze, Joel suddenly had to turn away. He wished Tony would be more careful.

Beyond all reason he also wished, as he often had before, that Tony were his brother. They could be twins . . . the kind that didn't have to look alike or *be* alike either. With so many other kids in the family, the Zabrinskys wouldn't miss Tony. If they needed a replacement, Joel would gladly trade Bobby-the-Whiner.

"You realize," Joel said, "that it's going to be a long walk up that hill."

Tony straightened up and grinned, his teeth bright against his already tanned skin. "We don't

---

14

have to go to Starved Rock," he said. "Maybe I've got a better idea."

"Better than Starved Rock?" Was there a chance he wasn't going to have to argue with Tony about climbing the bluffs?

Tony did a little jig next to the bridge railing as if he could explain himself that way. "We've got lots of time. We can do anything we want."

"Sure we can!" Joel agreed enthusiastically.

"We could even go swimming."

Joel couldn't believe his luck. "All *right*!" he exclaimed, holding out the flat of his palm for Tony to slap.

Tony ignored the gesture and instead bowed, extending a hand in the direction of the reddish brown water slithering far beneath the bridge. "It's a great day for swimming," he said.

Joel stared. "In the river?" he demanded. "You want to go swimming in the river?"

Tony shrugged elaborately. "Where else?"

"You might as well go swimming in your toilet."

"Who says?"

"My dad says! That's who."

"'My dad says,'" Tony mimicked, his voice coming out high and girlish.

Joel decided to ignore the taunt. He decided,

also, not to remind Tony of the promise he had been required to make to his father before they left. "You know we're not allowed to swim in the Vermillion. Nobody is. It's dangerous . . . sink holes and currents. Whirlpools, sometimes! Besides being dirty."

"Alligators, too, I bet." Tony was suddenly solemn, though his eyes still danced. "The red in the water probably comes from all the bloody pieces of swimmers the 'gators leave lying around."

"There's no alligators in the Vermillion! Do you think I'm stupid or something?" Joel could feel his face growing hot, despite the fact that he knew Tony was only teasing. "And the color just comes from clay, red clay."

"That does it!" Tony said, crossing his arms and pulling his T-shirt over his head. "If there's no 'gators and no blood, I'm going swimming for sure."

Leaving Joel's Schwinn still perched haphazardly against the railing, he went whooping the length of the bridge and crashed through the underbrush along the side of the road. He was swinging his pale blue shirt over his head like a lasso.

"Come on, Joel," he yelled back. "The last one in's a two-toed sloth!"

———

CHAPTER THREE

JOEL WATCHED TONY YELLING AND FLAILING his arms as he ran down the steep hill to the river. He shook his head. That patch of shiny green leaves halfway down that Tony was romping through was probably poison ivy.

He glanced over at his bike. Tony hadn't even bothered to hide it in the weeds along the side of the road. Joel propped Tony's old bike against the railing and wheeled his own off the bridge, laying it gently in the weeds beneath the structure. He considered, for a moment, leaving Tony's bike right where Tony had left his, out in the open where anybody could steal it. He didn't, though. If Tony's bike got stolen, he might never get another.

Swimming in the Vermillion! Of all the crazy ideas! Maybe even crazier than climbing the bluffs. Joel shook his head as he laid Tony's bike next to his own; then he started down the hill.

"You see what I mean?" Joel said when he arrived next to Tony on the riverbank. "It's really dirty. And the worst of the stuff, chemicals and sewage, you can't even see."

Tony ignored him, stripping off his jeans and his underwear. He had already dropped his shirt and kicked his sneakers off before Joel arrived. "It's wet, isn't it?" he asked.

"Like I said," Joel replied, "so's your toilet."

Tony stepped into the river at the edge, and the dirty water lapping over his feet made them disappear entirely. He turned back to Joel and grinned. "Not enough water in my toilet. I tried it once to see."

"You would," Joel replied. He wanted to sound grumpy, but he could feel the answering smile breaking through.

"You coming in?" Tony called back when the water swirled around his knees.

"I'm waiting for you to drown," Joel answered. "I just want to see it so I can tell your folks."

"Keep them from worrying," Tony tossed back.

"Keep your mom from waiting supper," Joel replied.

They both laughed then, and when the laughter had faded, Tony said, "Well, are you coming in, or are you just going to stand there and gawk?"

"Who's gawking?" Joel pushed one sneaker off with the toe of the other. "You're nothing to look at."

The water was just right, cool enough to raise gooseflesh at first but not cold enough to be numbing. The flow past Joel's legs felt like a refreshing massage. He hadn't realized, though, that the current was so strong. It seemed as though the water were barely moving when he looked down from the bridge.

"Watch out for the current," he called to Tony, standing several feet upriver from him.

"Agh!" Tony cried, grasping himself by the throat with both hands. "The current! It's got me. It's going to suck me under. It's going to swallow me up!" And he toppled over backward, howling. His head disappeared beneath the foaming water he churned up.

Joel stood where he was, waiting. When Tony stood up, he was a prehistoric monster emerging from a swamp. Joel could tell that was what he was by the way he stood, water streaming down his face, arms hanging low, head hunched forward.

"Come on," Joel said. "If we're going to swim, let's go back to the pool. It'll be better there."

Tony straightened up. "Why? This is fun!"

"But there's a sliding board at the pool. And there's other kids, too."

"Who needs a sliding board . . . or other kids?" Tony replied. "Besides, I'm swimming now." And he plunged into the water, face first this time, but thrashing just as much as before.

"Doesn't look like he even knows how," Joel muttered to himself, but then he wiped away the idea. It seemed disloyal. Tony went to the pool with him now and then, and he did the same things everybody else did. They spent most of their time going down the slide into shallow water or splashing one another.

Joel eased himself deeper into the water and dog-paddled a few strokes. He didn't want to put his face down to swim properly. He'd take the artificial blue of a pool and the sting of the chlorine any day. The river smelled of decaying fish.

"Maybe we ought to come down here every day,

work out. We could be on the swim team next year in junior high," Tony was saying.

Joel stopped trying to swim and stood up. "We'd get caught for sure if we started coming down here every day."

"Who's to see us?" Tony asked.

"I don't know, but somebody would. Somebody driving over the bridge, probably." Joel looked up toward the highway bridge, but there were no cars in sight.

Tony shook his head. "Sometimes, Bates, you sound just like your old man."

Joel could feel the heat flooding his face. "What's wrong with that?"

"'Be careful in that tree, son,'" Tony mimicked, "'you might get hurt. Watch Bobby when he crosses the street. Those drivers never pay any —'"

Joel had been moving closer to Tony as he spoke, and now he gave him a hard shove. Tony was expecting it, though, and he didn't even step backward. He countered with a push of his own.

Joel swung his arms to keep his balance, and he felt the bubble of anger that had been with him all morning expand inside his chest. What right did Tony have to make fun of his father? "At least my dad doesn't go around hitting kids with a belt," he said, stepping closer to Tony and clenching his fists.

Tony went white around the mouth, and Joel was instantly sorry that he had picked on Tony's father. He didn't know that Mr. Zabrinsky had ever really hit Tony with a belt anyway. He had only seen him take off after Tony once, snaking his belt out through the loops with one hand and holding his pants up with the other. Actually, Joel had thought it was kind of funny at the time . . . in a scary sort of way.

Tony took a wide swing at the side of Joel's head. Joel ducked it easily. Tony was bigger and heavier than he was, but he was slower, too.

For a moment they stood glowering at one another, breathing hard, their fists raised; then Tony turned and began to slog through the water toward the riverbank.

"Where are you going?" Joel asked.

"To Starved Rock," came the reply. "I'm gonna climb the bluffs . . . by myself."

Joel's heart sank. He didn't especially want to bike back to town alone, and he certainly didn't want Tony climbing the bluffs by himself. "Aw, come on, Tony," he pleaded. "We can stay here. This is fun."

"Like swimming in your toilet," Tony replied without looking back.

Joel answered with the first thing that popped into his head — "Toilets aren't so bad" — and to show Tony that he meant it, he plunged into the water, immersing his face and taking several strokes so that when he stood up he was in front of Tony again.

Tony grunted. He still looked pretty mad. "You're just saying that because you're scared to climb the bluffs."

Again the irritation flared. "Who's scared?" Joel demanded. "You're the one who's scared. Why, I bet you wouldn't even" — he hesitated, looking around for something to challenge Tony with, something he wouldn't mind doing himself — "swim to that sandbar out there." He indicated a thin, dark island of sand rising out of the river about a hundred feet from where they stood.

Tony narrowed his eyes, gazed in the direction Joel pointed. "Why should I be scared of that?" he asked scornfully. "I'll bet the river doesn't get deeper than this the whole way." The water divided at Tony's waist in a sharp V.

"I'll bet it's deeper than this lots of places," Joel said. "River bottoms change. That's one of the reasons they're so dangerous."

———

23

"I wouldn't be scared even if it was ten foot deep."

Joel stepped closer. "You willing to swim it then?"

Tony's chin shot up. "Sure. Unless you're too chicken to swim it, too."

"We'll see who's chicken," Joel said.

CHAPTER FOUR

JOEL PUSHED OFF WITH A BREAST STROKE. After a few of those and a couple more dog paddles, he gave up and put his face down so he could swim properly. He kept his eyes closed underwater, though. Every few strokes he raised his head, glanced toward the sandbar, and realigned himself. The current was pushing him downstream, and if he wasn't careful he would miss the sandbar entirely.

He could hear Tony splashing wildly behind him, puffing and spewing water, his hands flailing. He couldn't figure out why he had never noticed what a poor swimmer Tony was before now.

Joel touched bottom for a moment to catch his breath, peering back toward the riverbank, wiping the water from his face and trying to forget how dirty it was. Tony came to an agitated stop behind him, and Joel faced him. "If you can't swim any better than that, you'll never make the swim team next year."

Tony's chest was heaving. He gasped for breath as if he had been swimming for miles. "That's why I want to work out every day. You and me. I'll get better. We both will."

"How about working out at the pool?" Joel asked, feeling reasonable and somehow older than Tony, the way he often did. "It's cleaner, and we won't get into trouble for going there."

"How about working out in the middle of Main Street?" Tony replied. "Then everybody can see." He was still breathing hard.

"What difference does it make if anybody sees?"

"All the difference in the world. Do you want Rundle and Schmitt noticing what we're doing? If they see, then they'll want to try out for the team, too."

"So . . . let them try out. Who cares?" Joel couldn't figure out what was going on. This wasn't like Tony. He was always everybody's friend. So much so that sometimes Joel couldn't help but feel a little bit jealous, wanting to keep Tony to himself.

Maybe Tony knew his form was bad, and he was embarrassed. He'd probably never had lessons at the Y like most of the kids, and the last thing in the world he was ever willing to do was admit that there was something he didn't know.

Joel could still remember the time Tony had claimed to be an expert at hang gliding. He'd jumped out of his upstairs window with a sheet tied to his wrists and ankles. Tony said, afterward, that the reason it hadn't worked was because he hadn't jumped from high enough. The doctor had said Tony was lucky to have gotten off with only a broken arm.

"Come on," Tony prodded. "You said out to the sandbar. Are you giving up?"

"You sure you'll make it?" Joel eyed his friend's still faintly heaving chest meaningfully. "You look pretty tired to me."

Tony gave him a shove, almost caught him off balance. "Swim," he commanded, and Joel plunged into the water and resumed swimming. Tony started beside him but immediately dropped behind. Joel could hear him, blowing and puffing like a whale.

It's not so bad, Joel said to himself, beginning

to get his rhythm, discovering the angle that made it possible to keep gaining against the current. Maybe Tony was right and this river swimming would be a good way to practice . . . now that his father had decided he was old enough to be allowed a bit of freedom.

He started the side stroke. He could watch where he was going better that way, keep tabs on how far he still had to go. He couldn't see Tony coming behind, but he didn't need to see him. He could tell he was there, because he sounded like an old paddle wheeler.

Only about twenty more feet. Joel caught a toehold in the bottom for a second to look ahead. The water foamed and eddied around the sandbar as if it were in more of a hurry there than other places. He put his head down and began the crawl, angling upriver against the current.

He was gasping for breath each time he turned his head. He wasn't really tired, though. A little nervous, maybe. In the pool the side was always nearby, something to grab on to. Still, he was a pretty good swimmer, and he was doing all right. He *might* be good enough for the swim team by the time he got to junior high in the fall.

He should have thought of practicing in the

river himself. It had been a good idea. Tony was full of good ideas. When they both reached the sandbar, he would apologize, tell Tony he was sorry for what he'd said about his dad. He'd tell him he was sorry about saying Tony would be afraid to swim a little ways, too.

"Made it," he called out, when his hand scraped bottom with his approach to the sandbar. He stood up. "And I beat you, too!"

There was no answer. Joel turned to check.

Behind him stretched the river, smooth and glistening, reddish brown, but there was no sign of Tony. There was nothing to indicate that Joel wasn't alone, hadn't come into the water alone to start with. Except, of course, he hadn't.

He started to walk back, pushing through the water impatiently, as though it were a crowd holding him back. "Tony," he yelled. "Where are you?"

A faint echo of his own voice, high like the indistinct mewing of a cat, bounced back at him from the bluffs, but there was no other reply. Joel kept walking forward, pushing against the wall of water.

Maybe Tony had turned back; maybe he was hiding in the bushes somewhere along the bank, watching him, waiting for him to come unglued.

———

"All right, Tony Zabrinsky. I know your tricks. Come out, wherever you are."

There was no answer, not even a giggle from the bushes or some rustling.

"Doggone you, Tony, if you mess with my clothes . . ." But he could see his clothes, the pile of them, lying where he had left them, his red T-shirt marking the spot.

"Tony!" He began to move forward in lunges, gasping for breath, half choking. Tony had to be hiding. He had to be just off to the side somewhere . . . laughing. There was no other possibility.

It was when Joel stepped off into the nothingness of the deep water, the river bottom suddenly gone from beneath his feet as if he had hit a black hole in space, that he knew. As he choked and fought his way to the surface, he understood everything.

Tony couldn't swim – not really – and Tony had gone under.

CHAPTER FIVE

JOEL TREADED WATER FOR ANOTHER FEW seconds, looking across the deceptively smooth surface of the river. There was nothing there, no faint difference in the appearance of the water, nothing to give a hint of danger. How wide across was the hole? Where did Tony go under? Would he still be where he went down, or would the current have carried him away by now? How long could a person be underwater and still live?

The questions came at Joel in a barrage, leaving no space for answers, if there were any answers.

There wasn't time to wait for them anyway. He made a lunging dive, pulling himself forward and under with both arms, his eyes open and smarting in the murky water. He couldn't see more than a few inches in front of his face, so he reached in every direction with his hands as he swam, feeling for an arm, a leg, a bit of hair. Anything! He found nothing until he touched something slimy and rotting on the bottom and sprang to the surface.

He ducked under the water again, reaching on every side, looking and feeling until the river sang in his ears and he burst through to the light, pulling raggedly for air.

The current would have pulled Tony downstream. He let the river carry him a few feet farther on and tried again.

Nothing.

When Joel dove for the fourth time, letting the current carry him farther from the shore, he found himself caught in the grip of that hurrying water. It sucked at him, grinding him against the silty river bottom. As he struggled to rise, grasping at the water with both hands as if he could pull himself up by it, his hand touched something solid.

Was it Tony, floating just above him? He thrashed toward the object, only to have the current draw it from his reach. Then he was swirling, spinning, being pulled toward the bottom again while a dark, boy-shaped object pivoted above him, facedown in the muddy water.

Tony was dead . . . dead! And he, Joel, was going to die, too. He couldn't breathe. His lungs were a sharp pain. The air came bursting from his chest like an explosion, and the water rushed in to take its place. The form that had ridden above him brushed against his arm, his side. It was rough, hard, no human body. It was a log. Joel grabbed hold, and his head broke through the light-dazzled surface just as the rest of his body gave in to limpness.

He lay for a few minutes, coughing, spitting water, being moved without any assistance on his part from the eddying whirlpool to the slower, straighter current close to the riverbank. When the river bottom came up to meet his feet, he stood.

The sky was an inverted china bowl above his head. A single bird sang from a nearby tree.

Shut up, Joel wanted to shout. *You just shut up*. But he didn't. He didn't say anything. Instead, he bent over double and vomited a stream of water. Strange that river water in small amounts looked clean.

Joel could see everything with a sharp, terrible clarity: the river water he vomited, the bare roots of a tree thrust above the water, the steady progress of the river toward . . . where did it go? Toward the Illinois River. And the Illinois River emptied into the Mississippi. Didn't it?

They had studied rivers in school, but he couldn't remember.

He looked around. Still nothing disturbed the smooth surface of the water, and nothing skulked along the bank, no hidden form. He might have been the only human being alive in the entire world.

If he found Tony, if he found him hiding somewhere on the bank, he would beat him to a bloody pulp. He would never speak to him again, never do anything with him again. It was a dirty trick, the dirtiest trick Tony had ever pulled.

A shiver convulsed Joel, though the sun was still bright and hot, and he began to move woodenly toward the spot where he had left his clothes. He would get dressed and —

He stood there over his pile of clothes. Tony's clothes were scattered on the ground, exactly where he had dropped them. Tony couldn't have gotten out of the water. Not even Tony would be running around stark naked . . . just for a joke! Joel turned back to face the river again, squinting against the sunlight that glinted off the rippling surface.

———

It wasn't possible. It couldn't be. It was all a terrible dream from which he would awaken any moment.

Far above him, a car rumbled across the bridge.

"Wait!" Joel screamed, coming out of the trance in which he had been standing over Tony's clothes. "Stop! Help!" He ran toward the bridge, flailing his arms, but the car was too far away for anyone to hear . . . to see. It moved smoothly up the hill on the other side of the bridge.

Joel stopped in his tracks, trembling, his teeth chattering in erratic bursts, then ran back to his clothes. He grabbed his jeans from the pile, letting his underpants and shirt tumble to the ground. His hands shook so violently that he could barely hold the jeans up to step into them. The heavy material stuck against his wet skin. He tried to stuff his feet into his sneakers, gave up, and began to run toward the highway, still struggling to fasten the jeans. There would be another car coming soon. There had to be.

As he ran, he paid no attention to where he stepped. He looked down once, after tripping and picking himself up, to see that his big toe was bleeding, but it might have been someone else's toe. He felt nothing. A thistle beneath his left foot only made him move faster . . . up the hill, his lungs pumping. The air seemed to hold him back exactly as the water had earlier.

By the side of the highway, he doubled over, vomited again, and then stood erect. He had to get help. Maybe Tony could still be saved if he got help. The road climbed away from the river on each side . . . empty . . . bare. There wasn't a single car or truck in view. The only movement anywhere was a black crow wheeling high in the sky.

Joel turned toward home and began to run blindly up the middle of the highway. He could feel the river just behind him, a presence, a lurking monster waiting to pounce. A monster that swallowed boys. Joel increased his speed, his heart hammering against his ribs, his bare feet slapping against the dark pavement.

CHAPTER SIX

JOEL WAS HALFWAY UP THE HILL BEFORE another car crested the rise at the top and started toward him. It was a big, old boat of a car, blue with silver fenders, a red and orange flame painted on the hood. Joel planted himself in the middle of the lane, waving his arms. The blue car swerved toward the opposite side of the road, and he lunged to stay in its path, determined not to let it get away. The car came to a screeching, vibrating halt, inches from his extended arms.

"What in the hell do you think you're doing?" the driver yelled. He was a teenage boy, probably eighteen or nineteen, with a lot of dark hair and bare, muscular arms.

"Please," Joel gasped, but then he couldn't say any more. He stood doubled over the car's hood, trying to catch his breath, trying to get the words past his throat. "Please," he repeated.

"The kid looks sick," a blonde girl said. She was sitting next to the boy, so close that she could have been sharing the driving. She leaned forward as she spoke, peering through the windshield at Joel.

"In the river," he managed to say, pointing. "Please, come."

"What's in the river?" the boy asked, attentive now. "What're you talking about?"

Joel shook his head, unable to speak again. His face felt numb.

"You mean somebody's drowning or something?" The boy leaned forward, gripping the wheel.

Joel nodded dumbly.

"Get in!" the driver ordered, reaching back and swinging the door open for Joel.

Joel stumbled around the car and slid into the backseat, pulling the door shut again. The blonde girl turned and stared, her mouth working methodically around a wad of purple gum. She looked scared.

The car started up with a screeching of tires,

barreled down the road, and skidded to a stop on the gravel shoulder just before the bridge.

"Who'd you say it is?" the boy demanded, already out of the car and jerking open Joel's door. "A friend of yours?"

"Yeah," Joel said, finding a bit of voice as he climbed out of the car. "His name's Tony."

"Where'd he go in?"

"I'll show you," Joel said, and he headed for the riverbank at a stumbling run. The bigger boy ran beside him, the girl next to the boy, her hands fluttering in front of her like large moths.

The sight of the river, the faint, dead-fish smell of it, made Joel's knees buckle when he got to the bank again. The boy grabbed his arm and held him up.

"Here?" he asked, setting Joel back on his feet.

"There's a place where it gets deep . . . right about there." Joel pointed in the direction of the spot where he thought Tony had gone down.

The boy pulled off his shirt. "How'd he get in there anyway?" he asked.

"We were swimming out to the sandbar, and when I looked back . . . he wasn't there. I . . . I tried to find him. I really did." Joel choked as he spoke, his chest heaving in something like a sob,

---

but he wasn't crying. His eyes were perfectly dry, and though he was shaking, his insides were frozen into a dead calm.

The boy had kicked off his shoes and his jeans. He stepped into the river, then paused, squinting at the muddy water.

"This his clothes?" the girl asked, approaching with Tony's blue shirt cradled in her arms as if she thought she had rescued Tony.

"Yeah," Joel answered, resisting an impulse to tell her to keep her hands off Tony's things.

The boy plunged into the water, skimming beneath the surface, humping up and diving more deeply still.

"You be careful," the girl called toward the place where her boyfriend had disappeared.

Joel and the girl stood side by side, waiting. Joel wondered for a moment if he should be back in the water looking, too, but the memory of the current pulling at him, holding him down, turned his legs to lead. He couldn't move toward the river again. The boy was going to find Tony, anyway. Joel was certain of it.

The first time the boy surfaced, Joel called out excitedly . . . "Tony!" But the teenager's hands were empty, and Joel stifled a second, more forlorn cry.

"The current probably took him that way," Joel called, pointing toward the bridge, and the boy nodded and ducked under again, swimming farther out this time and emerging downriver ten or fifteen feet.

He stayed with it, turning in every direction, diving again and again until his chest heaved and he staggered when he stood. His girl friend paced on the bank, cracking her gum steadily. "Be careful. Be careful," she said occasionally, more to the surrounding air than to her friend.

"You won't find anything there," she called desperately when he swam almost to the middle of the river once. "He wouldn't have gone that far out."

"But what if he did?" Joel demanded, and the girl didn't answer. She looked as though she were about to cry.

Joel stood on the bank and called helpful directions, but finally, despite Joel's encouraging suggestion to try "just a bit farther down," the boy began wading toward shore. His head was lowered so the water sheeting off his hair wouldn't drip into his eyes.

"You aren't quitting, are you?" Joel asked, the knowledge that he had quit already lying heavily in his gut.

"Yeah," the boy gasped, picking up his shirt and wiping his face with it. "I'm quitting."

"But you can't," Joel wailed. "You just can't!"

The boy shrugged. He spoke between deep, quavering breaths. "Look . . . do you know . . . how long . . . it takes somebody . . . to drown?"

Joel didn't answer. He hadn't thought about it. Besides, he didn't want to know.

"About five minutes, I'd say." The boy bent over, resting his hands on his knees. "About five lousy minutes!" More deep breaths. "Maybe even less."

Joel turned away, walked along the bank a few feet, but the boy's voice followed him.

The boy was beginning to breathe more normally now, and the words came out in larger clumps. "And how long was it before you even got me down here? Ten minutes? Fifteen?"

Joel couldn't respond.

"And do you know," the boy went on, straightening up slowly, "how hard it is to find anything in a river like this . . . how fast the current would pull somebody along? Maybe next week a body'll wash up at one of the dams . . . or next month."

"We're not looking for a body," Joel said, turning back fiercely. "It's Tony we're looking for!"

The boy used his shirt to shear the water off his

chest and arms. He shook his head. "Sorry, kid," he said.

Joel went rigid. What was this guy saying? Sorry? What was he sorry about? He didn't even know Tony.

"Dumb kids," the boy muttered as he tugged on his jeans. "You shouldn't have been swimming in the river in the first place. You both should have known better. Didn't anybody ever tell you how dangerous rivers are?" He stuffed his feet into his shoes, wrung his wet shirt out. "Well," he said, "you'd better finish getting dressed and come with me."

Now it was Joel who was beginning to have trouble breathing. "Where are you going?" he asked.

"To the police station." The boy's voice was harsh, angry, as if he blamed Joel for what had happened. "When somebody drowns, you've got to report it to the police."

When somebody drowns. The words reverberated through Joel's skull like a scream. But he only repeated, dully, "The police," and stared at his own feet. What would the police say? They would want to know what Joel and Tony had been doing in the river in the first place. They would want to know what Joel had done to lose his friend that way.

Maybe he could call his dad at work first . . . before he went to the police station. His dad would be good at explaining things. His dad would . . . what would he do? "You're on your honor, Joel." That's what he had said. "You'll be careful the whole way? You won't go anywhere except the park?" And now Joel had proved what his honor was worth, what *he* was worth.

"Come on, kid," the boy said, and though his voice was still rough, it wasn't unkind. He knew. He knew what sort of questions the police would ask, what Joel's father would say, and Joel could tell the boy was feeling sorry for him.

"No," Joel said, shaking his head vigorously and pulling on his shirt. "You go on. I've got my bike here. I'll go report it to the police. No sense you getting involved."

"He's right," the girl said. She held her chin up and spoke with authority, though there were tears running down her cheeks. "There's no sense. Besides, if we go back into town, I might get into trouble. I called in sick to work today, remember? To go with you." She placed an extended index finger in the middle of the boy's chest.

"But it's gotta be reported," the boy said, stubbornly. "And the kid's parents have to be told, too."

At first Joel thought the boy was talking about his parents, about telling his father and mother, but then he realized the boy meant the Zabrinskys. Joel hadn't thought about Tony's parents up until now. For an instant he imagined ringing the Zabrinskys' doorbell, and he saw Mrs. Zabrinsky, her face tired, her eyes already sad, coming to the door. When the door opened, though, it was Mr. Zabrinsky standing there, a heavy, leather belt in his hand. Joel could feel the cold sweat breaking out along his sides. If the police didn't get him, Tony's father would for sure.

"I'll go to the police," he said. "I promise."

CHAPTER SEVEN

JOEL LEANED INTO HIS BIKE, PUSHING AS hard as he could, almost running up the hill. His heart drummed in his ears. The boy and his girl friend were still sitting in their car, probably arguing about whether or not to go to the police. Their presence behind him in the road made the skin between Joel's shoulder blades and up the back of his neck feel tight and bunchy.

When the car finally pulled away, rumbled across the bridge and up the opposite hill, Joel quit pushing and dropped across the handlebars, gasping for breath. After a few moments he looked back. The car was gone. Heat wavered off the empty road.

He began to push his bike again, more slowly now. When he was three fourths of the way to the top, a small red car crested the hill and started toward him. Joel straightened up, freezing his features into what he hoped was an image of innocence, of nonchalance. Still, when the car passed, he had to turn away. If the people in the car got a good look at his face, they would know.

His mother had always told him that he was the worst keeper of guilty secrets in the world. When he was a little kid, if he walked past her with a snitched cookie in his pocket, she would take one look at his face and say, "Joel, what do you have in your pocket?"

Now everybody was going to look at him and say, "Joel, why did you go swimming in the river? Joel, what did you do to your best friend?"

And what kind of questions would the police ask? What would they guess without even asking?

Joel stopped in his tracks, his heart beginning to hammer again. He couldn't go back. He just couldn't!

He jerked his bike around, facing it down the hill and away from town, away from the police, the Zabrinskys, his parents. He climbed on, standing with all his weight on one pedal so that his rear wheel fishtailed as he moved out. This time he would build up enough speed to make it to the top of the other side of the valley without having to get off once to push.

His father had given him permission to ride his bike all the way to Starved Rock State Park. He was going to ride to the park.

A line of fire measured the tops of Joel's thighs. He pedaled steadily, glancing neither to the right nor to the left, images flashing through his brain. The woods at the park were dense. He could hide his bike easily . . . and then himself. Maybe he could even find a cave in the bluffs that he could stay in. He could live on berries and roots the way the Indians had done. They had hidden out on top of Starved Rock bluff to get away from an enemy tribe, but he couldn't do that. There were footpaths and fences on top of the bluffs now . . . tourists, too. Anyway, an enemy tribe had trapped the Indians up there, starved them to death, giving the park its name.

A semi roared past, the suction of the huge wheels tugging at Joel and at his bicycle. All he would need to do would be to loosen his grip. The truck would take care of the rest.

Joel stopped pedaling, steered onto the shoulder, and dropped heavily off the bike. What was he doing? Did he really think he was going to hide out? And if he found some place to hide in, how long could he stay? Until he grew up . . . or died? But it wasn't his fault, was it? Just because he didn't follow his father's orders, that didn't make what happened to Tony his fault.

His father was the one who had said it was all right to ride to the park in the first place. Joel hadn't even wanted to go.

And then there was Tony, crazy Tony, insisting on swimming in the river when he couldn't even swim that well.

Joel expelled a long breath. He felt lighter, somehow. He glanced both ways, then walked his bike across the road and started back in the direction he had come from. He would go home. That was where he belonged . . . no matter what had happened.

He began to pedal again, his bike in the highest gear so the least movement on his part propelled him the farthest. *Home,* the narrow tires sang against the pavement. *Home.*

There was one thing he needed, though. He needed to decide what to tell his parents – and the Zabrinskys – when they asked about Tony.

He could tell them . . . he could tell them that he and Tony had started to ride their bikes out to Starved Rock. He could tell them that Tony had stopped when they were crossing the bridge. It was so hot. The river was there . . . cool and wet. Tony wanted to go swimming.

It was the truth, wasn't it?

And then he could tell them how he'd tried to talk Tony out of going into the river. And he could explain that Tony wouldn't listen, because Tony never listened once he had made up his mind. But then Joel would remind his father of the promise he had made that morning. He would say that he told Tony he couldn't go down to the river with him.

He would tell how he had ridden on to Starved Rock by himself. The day was hot, though, and it wasn't much fun riding so far without Tony, so he'd turned around to come back.

The explanation assembled itself in Joel's mind, logical and complete. Why hadn't he thought of it before? What had made him run away? He loosened his clenched fingers, one at a time, from the handlegrips and kept pedaling toward home.

But when he arrived at the top of the ridge overlooking the Vermillion River again, he stopped and stared at the road, the bridge, the wall of trees nearly obscuring the water. If only there were some other way to get home. He didn't know another route into town, though. Besides, the fire in his thighs had moved into his calves, his shoulders were cramped, and any other route home would undoubtedly be longer than this one.

Joel squeezed the hand brakes and began to creep down the steep hill toward the bridge, the brake pads squealing lightly against the wheels.

Tony had stayed behind to go swimming. That was what Joel would tell everybody. But if he had really ridden on to Starved Rock when Tony had gone down to the water, he would have stopped to check on Tony on the way back . . . because he wouldn't know.

Joel reached the bridge, still holding the bike in tight control, and pedaled slowly across, keeping his eyes carefully on the road. At the other side, though, he hesitated, stopped, wheeled his bike down the embankment, and propped it against the understructure of the bridge. He would just check . . . so people wouldn't look at his face when he explained and know he hadn't even checked.

Tony's BMX was still there, carefully obscured in the long grass.

Joel walked slowly toward the riverbank, keeping his mind carefully blank. The whole thing *could* have happened the way he had it figured out. It all made sense.

A squirrel scolded in a nearby tree. The river made a burbling sound, almost as if it were laughing.

There were Tony's clothes scattered haphazardly along the ground, exactly where they had been dropped except for the shirt the girl had moved. One sock hung from a nearby bush; the other lay in the midst of a patch of violets.

Sighing over Tony's carelessness, Joel gathered up the clothes, folded them, put them into a neat pile. He folded the pale blue shirt last and laid it on top of the rest, then surveyed the results of his work.

Something was wrong. Tony had never folded his clothes in his life, not unless his mother was standing over him anyway. Joel reached down and mussed the shirt.

As he straightened up, the gleaming surface of the water caught his gaze. The river was unchanged, innocent.

For an instant Joel couldn't breathe. His throat closed, and the air was trapped in his chest in a painful lump. He lifted his hands in surprise, in supplication, but when the breath exploded from him again it brought with it a bleating moan.

Joel stood on the bank clutching at himself and swaying.

Tony was dead . . . dead.

———

CHAPTER EIGHT

"Joel!" The angry voice came immediately after the slammed door. "Joel, where are you?"

Joel lay on his back in the middle of his bed staring at the darkened light fixture. The shadow of the fixture stretched across his ceiling like an elasticized gray spider and bent down the wall. When he had first lain down on the bed, the shadow had been a small blob right next to the light.

"Joel, are you up there?" came his father's voice again, and Joel shook his head slowly from side to side.

No, he wasn't up here. He wasn't anywhere. Hadn't Mrs. Zabrinsky told his father that? All afternoon the telephone had rung at frequent intervals. Then the doorbell. Ding-dong. Ding-dong. Knock, knock, rattle, rattle. First Bobby calling, obviously sent across the street by Mrs. Zabrinsky, then Mrs. Zabrinsky herself. "Joel! Tony!"

But the house key was in Joel's pocket, and no one could get in . . . except his parents when they got home from work. They had their own keys. Joel had lain there through the long afternoon and waited for one of them to get home. He had thought it would be his mother who would get there first, though. She usually did get home before his dad because she started work earlier in the morning.

The papers for his route had been dropped on his front porch about two hours before. He had heard the thunk when they hit the concrete, but he hadn't been able to make himself get off the bed to do anything about them. *I could be gone on my route when they come home,* he had thought, but still he hadn't moved.

"Joel!" His door shot open with a report like a firecracker and, as if connected to the door by a spring, he leaped off the bed. The blood rushed from his brain with the sudden movement, and he swayed giddily in the middle of his floor.

"So you *are* here. Mrs. Zabrinsky thought you were."

Joel didn't say anything. He studied a spot on the floor in front of his father's feet.

"What are you doing, locking yourself in the house all day? What do you mean by this kind of behavior?"

Joel's gaze traveled to his father's belt buckle.

His father was now looking around the room. "Where's Tony?" he asked. "Mrs. Zabrinsky said you two boys spent the entire afternoon locked in the house."

"Tony's not here," Joel said.

"Where is he, then?"

Joel gave a small shrug.

His father ran his fingers through his hair in exasperation. "What's going on, Joel? This isn't like you . . . sneaking into the house, leaving Tony's mother to worry." He took a step toward Joel, but Joel didn't flinch.

He looked into his father's face, waiting for the blow that he was sure would come . . . must come. His father had never hit him, but he would now. "I guess I fell asleep," he said. "I didn't hear a thing." He spoke out of the deep calm that had taken hold of him sometime in the long afternoon.

———

"Besides," he added, "it's my house. I can come here if I want to."

Now! His father would hit him now!

Joel's father quit tugging on his hair and dropped his hand. "Of course it's your house," he said quietly, "but you don't have permission to lock yourself in here when Mrs. Zabrinsky is supposed to be looking after you. She wouldn't have even known you were here if Bobby hadn't caught a glimpse of you going through the door."

"Snoop," Joel said.

"What?" his father asked, beginning to look exasperated again.

"Never mind."

"Well, where is Tony, then? His mother will want to know."

In the river, Joel thought, but out loud he said, "On the road to Starved Rock."

His father tipped his head to one side. He looked skeptical. "Alone?" he asked.

"I came back," Joel said. "Starved Rock was too far, so I came back." Was this what he had planned to say? He wasn't sure.

Bobby appeared in the doorway, his fists cocked on his hips in imitation of their mother's favorite stance when she was cross with either of them.

"You guys aren't supposed to be in the house when Mommy and Daddy are gone," he said in his best boy-you're-going-to-get-it voice.

"So what?" Joel snapped back and, instantly deflated, Bobby ducked his head, tucking his thumb into his mouth.

Joel's father was studying his face minutely. "You mean to tell me," he said, "that Tony rode all the way to Starved Rock by himself?"

"I guess he did," Joel said.

"He lied to me, you know, about his mother's giving him permission to go. I found that out from Mrs. Zabrinsky, too."

Joel could feel his father's gaze like a burning pressure. He held his breath, waiting for the moment when all would be known . . . but his father only shook his head, looked away. "I feel responsible. . . ."

You are responsible, Joel wanted to say. But instead he asked, his voice dull and flat, "Do you want me to go see if I can find him?"

"No, of course not." His father sighed. "It's too far to go back on your bike. Anyway you need to get started on your paper route." He turned and started out of the room, calling back over his shoulder, "I'll telephone the Zabrinskys and tell them that Tony will probably be late."

———

Very late, Joel thought, and he had a strange urge to laugh. *Tony's dead! Don't you know that?* he wanted to yell. But since it was obvious his father didn't know, that his father didn't know anything, he kicked the leg of his bed and muttered, "Frigging newspapers!"

Bobby's eyes grew round, but his father, though he must have heard, didn't turn back. He wasn't going to *do* anything, no matter what.

"Can I help you with your route today, Joel?" Bobby asked. Bobby was always wanting to help him with his route, with his Scout projects, with anything he did. Sometimes Bobby even helped him when it was his turn on dishes. Dumb little kid.

Joel didn't usually let Bobby go along on his route, though. Tony went along lots of times, but he had his own bike. Balancing Bobby on his bike along with the load of papers was a real trick.

Besides, Tony really helped. He didn't just tag along asking questions and getting in the way.

Tony! Would the Zabrinskys ever find him? The teenager had said something about a body maybe washing up at one of the dams . . . next week, next month. Maybe. Why hadn't Joel told his father about Tony's going down to the river to swim, about his going on to Starved Rock while Tony went to the river? Then his father could tell the Zabrinskys and the Zabrinskys would know where to look. Somehow nothing had come out right.

"Can I, Joel? Please?" Bobby repeated, and when Joel looked down at his brother, at the eagerness in Bobby's upturned face, his throat closed, and he had to turn away.

"Yeah," he managed to croak, "I guess you can help with my route today."

"Whoowee!" Bobby yelled, and he clapped his pudgy hands and skittered out of the room and back down the stairs.

Joel squared his shoulders and took a deep breath. Then he stopped, breathed again, sniffed. What was that smell in the air? Almost like . . . almost exactly like dead fish. Joel sniffed his arm, his shirt. That's where it was coming from . . . him.

Joel drew the neck of his shirt up over his nose and inhaled deeply. There was no question. The stink of the river had followed him home . . . and his father hadn't noticed that either.

Joel pulled the shirt off, got another from the drawer. The new shirt was fresh — it smelled like his mom's fabric softener — but the light fragrance couldn't cover the stench of the river clinging to his skin.

Joel started down the steps. Maybe nobody knew what a river smelled like.

Bobby was holding the screen door open for their mother. Looking tired and a little bit frazzled, she set down the grocery bag she was carrying and came to the bottom of the stairs. She stood with her hands on her hips exactly the way Bobby had when he was imitating her earlier. "What on earth were you doing today, Joel? Mrs. Zabrinsky says you and Tony hid in the house all afternoon."

Joel closed his eyes. It was going to start all over again. That was the problem with having two parents. You never heard anything only once. He drew in his breath, composed his face, and continued down the stairs. There was nothing he could do about the smell. "Tony wasn't here," he said, "and I wasn't hiding. I was lying down."

"Lying down?" Joel's mother reached to feel his forehead. "What's the matter? Are you sick?"

"No," Joel answered, submitting to the cool hand pressed to his head, "just not feeling good for a little bit."

"What did you and Tony do today?" his mother asked, her other hand circling the back of his head as though she could feel his temperature better by pressing with both hands. Her eyes were on his face.

"Just rode our bikes." The musky river smell was so strong it made his eyes burn. She had to smell it. There was no way she could miss it.

"How far did you go?"

Joel jerked free, ducking and coming up a few feet down the hall with his back to his mother. "Not very far. Tony was going to ride out to Starved Rock – Dad said we could – but I didn't feel good, like I told you, so I came home."

He couldn't tell what she was doing, behind him as she was, and he didn't want to turn around to look.

"Starved Rock," she repeated. "But that's so far!"

"Dad gave us permission," he said. And then he amended, "He said *I* could go."

"Well" – a light sigh – "you'd better get busy with your route before people start calling. They'll be complaining about their papers being late."

Joel felt his body go limp. His mother hadn't smelled the river. She hadn't even guessed he was lying. Relief swirled in his brain, curiously mixed with anger. Didn't anybody around here pay attention to anything?

He pushed out the screen door, letting it slam behind him . . . hard.

CHAPTER NINE

Bᴏʙʙʏ ᴡᴀs sǫᴜᴀᴛᴛɪɴɢ ᴏɴ ᴛʜᴇ ᴘᴏʀᴄʜ ᴏᴠᴇʀ the stack of newspapers, tugging on the twine that held them, his small, dirty fingers making little headway against the knot.

"You cut it, dummy," Joel said, pulling out his pocket knife. "Like this." He cut the twine on the papers and also on the stack of inserts next to them, his hands moving with angry impatience.

Bobby watched, his lower lip poking out. "You know I don't got a knife."

"Don't *have*," Joel corrected gruffly, looking away from Bobby's face. "You don't *have* a knife."

"Well, I don't," Bobby said, and he grabbed an advertising circular and stuffed it inside a paper, crumpling both.

"Take it easy," Joel ordered, thumping Bobby on the top of the head with the handle of his knife. "You're going to mess everything up."

Bobby's face rumpled, and he began to cry. "That hurt!" He rubbed the top of his head.

"Everything hurts," Joel mumbled, but now the anger was replaced by shame. What was he on Bobby about? The poor little kid was only trying to help. Joel began pulling the circulars off the stack, one at a time, snapping them into place inside the fold of the papers, rolling the papers to ready them for throwing. *Everything hurts,* he repeated to himself, *except maybe being dead. Being dead's probably the only thing that's easy.*

The thought made his skin go cold and tingly.

"What's wrong, Joel?" Bobby asked. "Why do you look like that?" His own pain forgotten, Bobby was staring with enormous green eyes.

"Nothing," Joel said, but the word came out sounding squeezed. "If you're going to help, start putting the papers in the bag."

Bobby began bagging the papers, but he didn't take his eyes off Joel's face.

"Watch what you're doing," Joel snapped, pulling the anger around himself again like a cloak. "We've gotta get this show on the road."

———

Bobby nodded sharply and set to loading the rolled papers into the bag as fast as Joel could get them ready.

Joel stuffed and rolled, the fury taking over again, but this time he knew whom he wanted to punch. It was all Tony's fault. All of it! Tony knew what a poor swimmer he was. He had to have realized the risks. And now he had gone off and left Joel to answer for him. And what was he going to say?

Tony's parents would probably be asking questions by the time he got home from his route. *Tony isn't home, Joel. Where could he be? You're the last one who saw him . . . alive.*

"Damn it all, anyway!" Joel cried, pushing the rest of the stack of papers off the porch. "I'm sick of this stinking paper route."

Bobby was sitting back on his heels, his eyes in danger of swallowing up his face. He peered over the edge of the porch and then up at Joel. "You squashed three of Mommy's purple things," he said.

Joel looked, too. The papers were lying in the middle of his mother's petunia bed.

"Do you want me to get the papers back?" Bobby asked. "I think if we brush them off they'll still be okay."

"All right," Joel consented. "Get them back."

Bobby climbed down the steps and then up again. He peered cautiously over the stack of papers he carried. "They're okay, Joel," he said, laying them down reverently, as though they were jewels.

Joel shook his head, trying to dispel the red fog that had taken possession of his brain. If he could get his hands on Tony now, he would . . . But that was ridiculous. What would he do? What could anybody do? Beat Tony up?

At the thought he let out a choking guffaw, half laughter, half sob.

Bobby was watching him again, his face wary, his lower lip clenched between small, white teeth. "Are you okay, Joel?" he asked.

"Yeah," Joel said. "I'm okay." He went back to preparing the papers. "I'm alive, aren't I?"

The paper route seemed endless. Bobby rode behind Joel on the bicycle seat and chattered the whole way. Joel tried to listen, with half an ear anyway, but he couldn't. With each thunk of a paper on a porch, he heard, instead, Tony's voice, challenging, teasing. "I'll bet you can't get one in the middle of Mrs. McCullough's hanging geraniums. I'll bet you can't clip the Smiths' cat. Why don't you . . . ?"

Joel wanted to yell at Tony, to tell him to shut up, but even Bobby would think he was crazy if he started yelling at a voice inside his own head.

Why did he feel so *responsible,* as though he had pushed Tony in? Why did he always have to feel responsible for *everything* that happened? If they had gone climbing on the bluffs and he, Joel, had fallen, Tony wouldn't have blamed himself. Would he?

Tony had said once that Joel was like an old grandmother, fretting all the time. Well, Tony ought to see him now. He would laugh.

At the thought of Tony laughing, Joel almost smiled. He and Tony always had so much fun together. Besides the tree house they were building this summer, they had a lot of other projects going. They always did.

For one thing, they had been pooling their allowances to buy a worm farm. Their plan was to get rich selling bait. Tony had even had the idea of using his mother's meat grinder to grind whatever worms were left at the end of the summer and sell them as goldfish food. (That was because Joel's father had pointed out that neither family would want worms multiplying in the basement over the winter.) For his part, Joel was skeptical about whether there were very many people anxious to buy worm mash for goldfish food, but he hadn't said that to Tony.

Last summer they had concocted a wonderful scheme for getting rich selling decorative pennies. They flattened fifty pennies by leaving them on the tracks to be run over by the 3:45 train, turning them into thin, coppery disks. Their plan hadn't been exactly what anybody could call successful, though. They sold only one penny, because every other kid in town knew how to flatten pennies, too. The one they sold (for a nickel) was to a prissy girl whose mother wouldn't allow her to go near the tracks. They had been left with forty-nine pennies they couldn't spend, not even in a gumball machine.

Joel tossed the last paper and turned his bike toward home. Bobby had finally fallen silent, and Joel was grateful for that. He could feel his brother's small, hot hands gripping his shirt and the puffs of breath on the back of his neck, so close, so alive.

A surge of protectiveness passed through Joel. He would have to teach Bobby how to swim.

Bobby was afraid even to get his face in the water. Joel would start working with him right away. Every kid needed to know how to swim. Sometimes parents didn't seem to realize what a dangerous place the world is.

When Joel turned the corner by his house, he could see his mother and father in the front yard, talking to Mr. and Mrs. Zabrinsky. Seeing the four of them standing there, their faces solemn and intent, sent a chill through Joel's bones. What were they talking about? What did they know? By now, someone must have seen through his lie.

Or maybe the teenage boy had come back and turned Joel in.

Joel coasted up the driveway and stepped off his bike, pushing it into the garage before Bobby had a chance to climb down. Inside the garage, he scooped Bobby off the seat and set him on the floor.

"Thanks, buddy," he said. "I appreciate your help." He propped his bike along the wall, out of the way of the cars.

"I'll help you again tomorrow, Joel," Bobby said, his face glowing in the semidarkness of the garage.

"We'll see," Joel said, patting Bobby's shoulder.

He began tinkering with his bicycle, shifting the gears back and forth uselessly, pretending to be engrossed.

Bobby watched him for a moment, then turned and headed outside with a one-legged skip. "Mommy, Daddy," he called before he was even beyond the front of the garage. "Joel's gonna let me help him with his paper route tomorrow, too."

Joel stood where he was, trying to control the way his hands trembled, the way the muscles in his face seemed to jerk. They were talking about *him* out there. He was certain of it. But there was no way past them without being seen, and if he stayed in the garage any longer, they would probably notice that, too. He shifted the gears one last time, slumped his shoulders, and pulled his head in, like a turtle retreating into its shell. Then he stepped out into the staring light of the driveway.

CHAPTER TEN

"JOEL, WOULD YOU COME HERE FOR A MOMENT, please?" Joel's father called.

Joel hesitated, wondering if he dared pretend he hadn't heard, but then he turned slowly and, keeping his head down, moved in the direction of his father's voice.

"The Zabrinskys want to know where you saw Tony last," his father said when he had arrived at his side.

Joel had a sudden image of Tony laughing, the river water streaming from his dark hair. "On the road," he said. "On the road to Starved Rock."

"But where on the road?" Mr. Zabrinsky asked. "How far had you boys gone before you turned back?" Mr. Zabrinsky was a big man, with huge, rather hairy hands. He sounded impatient.

"Oh," Joel said, scuffing the head off of a dandelion with the toe of his sneaker, "about as far as the bridge over the river, I guess."

"The bridge over the river!" Mrs. Zabrinsky repeated with a small gasp.

Mr. Zabrinsky leaned toward Joel. "But he was on his way to Starved Rock. Right?"

"Right," Joel mumbled, wishing, again, that he had remembered the first time to tell the story he had originally planned.

"Besides," Mrs. Zabrinsky said, "Tony can't swim. He'd know better than to go near the river." She seemed to be trying to reassure herself.

"He can't swim?" Joel asked, squinting up at her. "Really?"

She smiled, a crooked half smile that Joel had seen a million times. "You must know that, Joel. You've gone to the pool with him . . . when he's willing to go."

Joel shrugged, tried to look away. "Well, he mostly played on the slide – or on the ropes, you know? – but he never told me he couldn't swim."

Mrs. Zabrinsky touched Joel's arm, and without thinking he jerked away. His skin felt clammy, and he was sure the stink of the river rose from him like a vapor.

"Maybe I shouldn't have told you," she said. "Maybe he wouldn't want you to know. He tried swimming lessons once, but he was always afraid of the water."

Tony? Afraid? Joel pushed the thought away.

"Is that all?" he asked, stuffing his hands into his pockets.

"Yes," his father said. "I guess that's all." And as Joel walked away, trying to look casual, trying to remember how his feet used to move when he wasn't thinking about them, his father added to the Zabrinskys, "Let's call the park ranger. If he doesn't know anything, then we should probably drive out there, take a look for ourselves."

"I suppose I shouldn't worry," Mrs. Zabrinsky replied, "but you know what Tony's like. I guess I worry more about him than all the rest of the kids rolled up together."

Joel stepped through the front door into the cool darkness of the hall. Why hadn't Tony thought about his mother, about the way she worried, before he had decided to go for a swim?

Joel stood in the shower, the water streaming over his skin. He had soaped three times, his hair, everything, and rinsed and soaped again. The water was beginning to grow cool, so he would have to get out soon. His mother would be cross with him for using all the hot water.

He turned off the shower, toweled dry. As he rubbed his skin, the smell rose in his nostrils again, the dead-fish smell of the river.

He considered getting back into the shower, but he didn't. It wouldn't help. He knew that.

He pulled on his pajama bottoms and walked through the dark hall to his bedroom. Bobby was in bed, probably already asleep. Lights were on downstairs, and the murmur of his parents' voices floated up the stairwell. They were talking about Tony, of course. What else?

He didn't turn on a light in his room. He simply headed for the dark shape of his bed and lay down on top of the spread, arranging his arms and legs gingerly, as if they pained him.

After a while he heard light footsteps on the stairs, and then his mother came into his room. She sat down next to him on the bed, so close that he knew she had to be pretending not to be offended by the smell.

"Joel," she said, "are you sure you've told us everything you know?"

"About what?" he demanded roughly, as if he

didn't understand what she meant, wishing it were possible not to understand.

"About Tony, about what you boys did today."

For an instant he thought about telling her. It would have been such a relief to let the words spill out, to let the choking tears come. But then he thought about having to tell the Zabrinskys, too, and the police, and about the twisted disappointment in his father's face, and he couldn't. He simply couldn't. He flopped over onto his stomach, muffling his response with the pillow.

"I already told you. . . . I got tired and came home. I don't know what Tony did."

"Did you boys have a fight?" she asked gently.

Joel remembered being mad at Tony, but he couldn't remember, now, why he'd been mad. Especially he remembered saying, "You're the one who's scared."

"No," he said. "We didn't have a fight."

His mother continued to sit there, as though she expected him to say more, and after a while Joel began to hold his tongue tightly between his teeth. It was the only way he knew to hang on to the words that threatened to come tumbling out of his mouth. *I know where Tony is,* he wanted to say. *I can tell you exactly where to begin looking.*

Finally his mother leaned over and kissed the back of his head, then got up to go. After she had left the room, Joel unlocked his jaws, relishing the burning pain in his tongue.

A few minutes later he heard his father's footsteps on the stairs, heard him stop just outside his room. He waited there for a long time, but Joel pretended to be asleep, lying perfectly still and concentrating on keeping his breathing steady and slow. Finally his father went away, too.

Joel buried his face in his pillow, pressing his nose and mouth into the suffocating darkness. It would have been better if he and Tony had tied themselves together and climbed the bluffs. At least he wouldn't have been left behind.

CHAPTER ELEVEN

JOEL LAY WAITING. HE STARED INTO THE darkness until his eyes ached, straining to see, to hear, though he didn't know what he was waiting for.

When he heard a sound at last, the soft swish of automobile tires on pavement, the hollow thud of doors closing, muted voices, he stood and moved quickly to his window.

A car had stopped in front of the Zabrinskys' house, and two men were walking up to their front door.

Joel gasped. Police! The men were police officers! The teenage boy must have reported him after all!

He tried to pull his jeans on over his pajamas,

but his foot got tangled in the fabric. He kicked the jeans out of his way and hurtled down the stairs. He had to explain! If the police found out from Mr. and Mrs. Zabrinsky about the lie he had told . . .

The front door was locked, and he lost precious seconds fiddling with it, jerking the lock this way and that until the door finally sprang toward him and he pushed the screen door out of his way. But at the edge of the porch, he stopped, caught his balance on the top step.

Across the street, Mr. Zabrinsky stood silhouetted in his front doorway, talking to the officers. Behind him, Tony's mother moved through the lighted hall toward the front door and the cluster of men. Joel's stomach twisted. He was too late.

He turned to go back inside, but the door opened and his father stepped onto the porch, buttoning a short-sleeved shirt. Joel looked to see if his mother was coming, too, but she wasn't. She must already have gone to sleep.

"Come on, son," his father said. "Let's see if there's anything we can do."

No! Joel wanted to whisper, to shout. *I'm not going over there.* Not a single sound came out of his mouth, though, and when his father put a hand on his shoulder, he seemed to lose all capacity to resist. He turned and walked with his father toward the Zabrinskys' house.

"Here's the boy who was with Tony," Mr. Zabrinsky was saying as Joel and his father joined the officers on the porch. Mr. Zabrinsky spoke without inflection. All the life seemed to have been squeezed out of his voice.

The two policemen pivoted simultaneously to face Joel, their eyes shadowed by the visors of their caps, their mouths set lines. One of them held a plastic bag from which he had drawn Tony's pale blue shirt. Joel stepped backward, but his father held an arm behind him. Joel couldn't tell if his father was protecting him or preventing him from running away.

"What have you found?" his father asked.

"The boy's clothes," the officer holding the shirt said. "By the river. His bike, too."

Joel stole a glimpse at Tony's mother. She was swaying, her hands pressed against her face. Did she know the truth? Did she know he had been there, that he had seen it all? He couldn't tell.

"Did you know Tony went down to the river, Joel?" Mr. Zabrinsky asked in the same lifeless voice he had used at first.

"No," Joel said. "I didn't know anything. I got tired, like I told you. I . . ." They were all looking at him, the police officers, Tony's parents, his father. Staring. Again Joel started to back away, and again his father's arm prevented him from doing so. The slight pressure of the arm along his back made him want to strike out, to break away and run. If he could get away, he could hide someplace where those terrible eyes couldn't follow. Why had he come back from Starved Rock? He couldn't seem to remember.

"Okay," he said. "Okay. Tony said he was going to go swimming. I tried to stop him. I told him the river was dangerous."

"And did you see him go into the water?" one of the officers asked, stepping closer to Joel.

The other one moved in closer, too, asking, "Were you there?"

"No!" Joel cried. "No!"

"Nobody's blaming you, son," the first officer said. "But the more you can tell your friend's parents" — he indicated the Zabrinskys with one hand as though directing Joel's attention to a picture or a statue in the doorway there — "the easier it will be. It's the not-knowing that's the worst."

"Please," Mrs. Zabrinsky whispered. "If you know anything . . ."

Mr. Zabrinsky leaned against the doorframe, one massive fist pressed tightly against his mouth, weeping silently.

"Joel?" his father said. "You've got to tell us." And then he turned to the others and added, laying his arm heavily across Joel's shoulders, "Joel is an honorable boy. He'll tell you what he knows."

Honorable! Joel staggered beneath the weight of his father's arm, then pulled away, teetering on the edge of the porch. The five faces bent toward him were like five pale moons, but it was his father's face that loomed the largest.

He took a deep breath. "Tony wanted to climb the bluffs at Starved Rock, and I was scared to do it. So when he changed his mind, when he decided to go swimming instead . . . I thought . . . I thought . . ." He was shaking all over as he spoke. "I looked for him. When he went under, I tried to find him. But I couldn't. . . . He just . . . he just . . . disappeared."

"Oh . . . Joel!" The arm that had been holding him didn't reach out to touch him again. "Joel!" his father repeated.

Mr. Zabrinsky moaned and stepped backward

into the shadowy hall. Tony's mother stood perfectly still. She didn't look at her husband. She stared only at Joel, her face twisted and ugly.

Everybody was looking at him, blaming him. He wanted to turn away, to run at last, but his feet refused to carry him in that direction. Instead, he stumbled toward his father, his hands raised and clenched into fists. "I hate you!" he cried, pounding at his father's chest. "It's all your fault. You never should have let me go!"

His father said nothing, did nothing to shield himself from Joel's fists. He simply stood there, absorbing the force of the blows until Joel could bear it no longer. He turned and leaped off the porch and bolted across the street.

But even as he slammed through the door and ran up the stairs to his room, he knew. It wasn't his father he hated. It wasn't his father at all.

He was the one. . . . Tony had died because of him.

CHAPTER TWELVE

JOEL LAY CURLED ON HIS SIDE, FACING HIS bedroom door. That's where his father would appear when he came to punish him. He would have to do it this time. He wouldn't have any choice.

He would punish him for yelling at him . . . for hitting him . . . for daring Tony to swim out to the sandbar.

Joel had known from the beginning that it was his fault. From the moment Tony had disappeared, he had understood. Running away hadn't changed a thing, and coming back hadn't changed anything either.

Nothing could change what had happened . . . ever.

A light summer breeze fanned across the bed, rustled the leaves on the maple tree outside his window. It was the tree Joel and Tony had been building a tree house in. The sound of leaves, the touch of cool air on his skin, was good. It was good to be able to feel such things, but Tony couldn't. Tony couldn't feel anything anymore.

Joel lifted his arm to his nose and sniffed. The smell was still there, so sharp that it made his eyes sting. He supposed it would be with him for the rest of his life.

Why had he been dumb enough to dare Tony, anyway? He knew what Tony was like. If somebody had dared him to walk through fire, he would have done that, too.

Joel pulled the pillow over his head, pushed it off again. His eyes were as dry and scratchy as sandpaper. He wished his father would come, get it over with.

The front door opened and closed again. Joel could hear his father fiddling with the lock. Didn't he understand yet? Bad wasn't something that could be locked out. Bad was something that came from inside you when you didn't even know it was there.

His father was moving up the stairs now, his

footsteps heavy and slow, and he stopped outside Joel's door as he had earlier in the evening. Joel lay quietly, holding his muscles rigid, although he knew pretending to be asleep wouldn't work this time.

His father came in. He pulled a chair away from Joel's desk, set it next to the bed, very close, and sat down. At first he didn't say anything, and Joel thought, *He's going to sit there all night. That's his way to punish me. He's going to sit there so I can't run away, so I can't sleep, so I couldn't even cry if I wanted to.*

Joel tried to keep his breathing steady and slow the way he had done before, but he felt as though he had been running for a long time and had to gasp for air. His skin was too tight. He was going to explode.

"I'm sorry," his father said finally.

"Sorry?" Joel blurted, astonishment rolling him over onto his back. "Why are *you* sorry?"

His father didn't answer at first, and just when Joel was convinced he wasn't ever going to answer, he said, "I'm sorry I misjudged the situation. I'm sorry I gave you permission to go."

Joel didn't respond.

"And," his father added softly, "I'm sorry that I

———

84

wasn't there to help you, that you had to be so frightened and so alone."

"It was my fault," Joel said dully. "The whole thing was my fault."

"Probably nobody could have found Tony in that water," his father replied, not understanding. "And if you had managed somehow, he might have pulled you under. He was bigger than you, heavier. He wouldn't have known what he was doing."

Joel thought of the swirling water closing over his head, pouring into his lungs, and his skin rippled into gooseflesh. But then he thought of Tony, Tony taking dibs on *his* bike, Tony dancing a jig on the bridge, Tony pretending to be a pre-historic monster. "It should have been me," he said.

Joel's father took hold of his arm, almost roughly. "Don't you say that," he said. "Don't you ever let me hear you say that."

Joel looked his father full in the face. "It's my fault," he repeated. "If I hadn't gone down to the river, Tony would have stayed out of the water."

"Maybe," his father said. "Maybe not. There's no way to know. You can't live your life by *maybe*s."

Joel's arm was beginning to hurt where his father

---

gripped it, but that wasn't enough. Nothing his father said or did was enough. "Are you going to punish me?" he asked.

His father sighed, was silent again for a moment, his hand gently smoothing away the earlier pressure. "Is that what you want?"

"You said I was on my honor this morning. I wasn't supposed to go anywhere except the park."

His father merely asked, "What would it teach you, son . . . more punishment?"

Since Joel had no answer for that, he said the only thing he could think of to say, said it harshly, as though it were an accusation. "Your hand is going to smell like it."

"Like what?" His father raised his hand to his face.

"Like the river. Don't you notice the stink?"

His father sniffed his hand again, bent over to bring his nose close to Joel's skin, then straightened. "I don't know what you mean, Joel. I can't smell anything."

"But *I* can smell it," Joel wailed. "It won't go away."

His father didn't say anything.

"Make it go away," Joel spoke in a whisper, as if they were discussing another person standing

86

in the room, someone who could be forced to leave.

His father smoothed the hair back from Joel's face. "I can't," he said, very quietly.

The anger surged through Joel's veins. He wanted to push his father away, to pummel him again. What good was this man who couldn't protect him from bad things happening and wouldn't punish him to make things right? "You don't understand," he said through clenched teeth. "I dared Tony to swim out to the sandbar. I knew he couldn't swim all that well. I must have known. And I dared him."

Joel expected . . . he didn't know what he expected, actually. Maybe he expected the world to fall in. At the very least he expected his father to rise up in rage. Instead there followed only another silence, the kind that made him want to scream. He held himself carefully rigid, though, and didn't move, only waited.

"It's going to be a hard thing to live with, for both of us," his father said at last. "But there is nothing else to be done."

Joel sat up. He was shouting now. "What are you talking about . . . we? *You* didn't do anything. You didn't even know you shouldn't have let me go!"

"But we all made choices today, Joel. You, me, Tony. Tony's the only one who doesn't have to live with his choice."

For a moment Joel could only stare, uncomprehending, at this man who wouldn't . . . couldn't take away his pain. Tony was free, while he, he and his father, would have to live with this terrible day forever. And though Joel clenched his jaw and squeezed his eyes shut, it was no use. He began to sob.

"Ah," his father said, as if relieved, and he leaned forward, drawing Joel onto his lap. Joel felt awkward, oversized. Surely there was no longer room for him here. But his father wrapped his arms around him tightly, and Joel's cheek settled into the hollow between his chest and shoulder. The racking sobs flowed out of him like water.

His father held him for a long time, saying nothing, until Joel's tears came without sound and his breaths were quivering gasps. Even then, his father held him. After a while, Joel began to pattern his breathing to match the steady rising and falling of his father's chest.

"I'd like to go back to bed now," he said finally. His father, instead of simply releasing him, reached forward to strip back the covers, then stood and laid him gently in the bed. He pulled the sheet up and tucked it beneath Joel's chin.

He will leave me now, Joel thought, but his father sat down in the chair once more.

Joel turned on his side, facing his father this time. He was tired, exhausted, but tinglingly awake. He was also empty, as though he had been hollowed out with a knife. He tried to think of something to say, if only to hear his father's voice.

"Do you believe in heaven?" he asked at last. "Do you believe Tony's gone there?"

His father bent toward him. "If there is a heaven, I'm sure Tony's gone there," he replied. "I can't imagine a heaven that could be closed to charming, reckless boys."

If! Joel felt as if he were sinking through the bed. "What do you mean . . . *if* there's a heaven?"

"I don't suppose anybody knows," his father answered gently, "what happens after." He hesitated, and one hand came up, described a series of circles in the air, then settled into his lap again as though it had finished the statement for him. "I believe there's something about life that goes on. It seems too good to end in a river."

Joel let his father's words sift through him slowly. He had hoped for something firmer, more certain.

Yes, there is a heaven. Certainly Tony is there now. He would have to settle, though, for what he got.

And what he got was a gentle summer night, a hollow place inside his gut that felt as though it might never be filled, and this man, his dad, who sat beside his bed.

"Will you stay?" he asked, reaching a hand out tentatively to touch his father's knee. "Will you sit with me until I fall asleep?"

"Of course," his father said.